Release

Copyright © K.I. Lynn

This book is a work of fiction. Names, characters, places, and incidents either are products of the author's imagination or are used fictitiously. Any resemblance to actual events or locales or persons, living or dead, is entirely coincidental.

This work is copyrighted. All rights are reserved. Apart from any use as permitted under the Copyright Act 1968, no part may be reproduced, copied, scanned, stored in a retrieval system, recorded or transmitted, in any form or by any means, without prior written permission of the author.

Cover image licensed by shutterstock.com/ ©Valua Vitaly, 123rf.com/ ©Frugo
Cover design by L.J. Anderson

Editors
Marti Lynch

Publication Date: April 23, 2016
Genre: FICTION/Romance/Erotica
ISBN-10: 1535409819
ISBN-13: 978- 1535409810
Copyright ©2016 K.I. Lynn
All rights reserved

RELEASE

by
K. I. Lynn

Intro

Our story was never rainbows and sunshine. It was gritty and raw, and a force neither of us were able to deter.

But that's what a true love is—an undeniable power—and that was exactly what captured us. As close to love at first sight as two fucked-up people could get.

It started with two broken people, and ended with a love worth dying for.

But love isn't perfect. Love isn't without sacrifice and struggle.

Especially with all that we've been through.

Chapter 1

Two years ago...

I took a drag from the cigarette in my hand and stared out at the dark loft apartment. Calm and quiet, with the exception of a little bit of noise from the street below. In the bed beside me, there was a passed-out brunette.

I didn't know her name. It didn't matter anyway—I was never coming back.

Little groans signaled she was waking back up, and that I'd missed my opportunity to leave.

She reached out and found my thigh, running her hand slowly up and then down.

"Mmm, baby, you really know how to pound a pussy."

Baby.

My stomach turned. A small term of endearment that could either be the first step of clingy, or the less likely—she forgot my name.

I would prefer the latter. Makes my never seeing her again easier.

A different woman every few weeks. They were nothing more than a human fleshlight.

A tool to get off.

"I have to go," I said as I snuffed out the cigarette.

Her hand fell from me as I stood so I could locate my clothes.

"So soon? Don't you want to go for another round first?"

"No." Any niceties, finesse, and chivalry I expressed when we met was gone. Exhaustion took over, and after a fuckfest, I no longer had the energy to keep the façade up.

She balked at me, mouth open and eyes wide before her anger and indignation exploded. She got up and turned the light on.

"Seriously? That's it?"

I pulled my shirt over my head, noticing the way her eyes widened at the large scar on my left side, and I slipped my shoes on.

"Yep."

Fuck and run.

Don't get close.

They're always watching.

"Asshole!" Her shrill scream echoed through the room as she lofted the nearest item—a pillow—at me.

A quick check for my wallet, keys, and phone, and then I looked at her.

"What? Did you think we'd run off into the sunset? Get married? All because you let me fuck you?"

She stared at me, her arms crossing over her chest. "Is a date really too much to ask for?"

I stepped around the bed, stopped right in front of her, and leaned down to run my tongue across her lips.

"Yes."

Matter of fact.

Had to be.

Break down any inkling of more.

There could never be more again.

She cocked her hand back, but I was too far away by the time she swung.

The curses aimed at me could still be heard as I shut the door and walked the few feet to the elevator. When the doors opened, I stepped on and leaned against the far wall, her shrieks drifting away as the doors closed.

How many was it now? Who knew. I stopped counting long ago.

As the anxiety, the PTSD, spiraled out of control, so did an insatiable sex drive.

The doors opened and I exited into the parking garage. Her hand was on my cock when we pulled in, so I couldn't remember where I parked. It took a few minutes and a lot of clicks on my fob before the lights on my sedan blinked.

Climbing in, I pulled out my phone. It was two in the morning, and I had three missed phone calls.

Before driving off, I looked at the call list—my parents. With a sigh I hit the button for voicemail.

"*You have two unheard messages,*" the automated voice said before playing the first one.

"*Nate, it's your dad.*" I shook my head and let out a small chuckle. He always started out that way, like I wouldn't recognize his voice. "*Just calling to remind you Erin's birthday is Saturday. We really hope to see you. Call me back when you get this. Love you.*"

Backing up, I drove out and headed home. I'd call him back in the morning, tell him I'd go, even though I didn't want to.

Family functions sent me into the worst panic attacks. Maybe I wouldn't go.

"*Hi Nate, it's Jack.*" My heart stopped before picking up into a furious tempo. My hands began to shake as my second father's voice came through the phone. "*It's been a while. You haven't been replying to my emails.*" Because I can't. Because I have nothing to say. "*I want to get together for lunch this week. I have a proposition for you. Call me… We miss you, son.*"

Son.

I clenched my hands around the steering wheel to stop the vibrations, to calm myself.

After everything, he still called me son. It stung. A burning sword of guilt to the gut compared to the pride it used to evoke.

I was the man that got his only daughter killed. The man who should have died.

My body held the scars to prove it.

I drove home, contemplating what he could want, and trying to decide when to call him back.

It wasn't like my days were filled with activity.

Get up, run, eat, smoke, go to the bar, fuck something or somebody, sleep—my daily routine when I could get out of bed.

For a year I'd rented a studio apartment over some stranger's garage. Contact with anyone I knew was a minimum. Family only if I had to.

Trapped in hell.

My wife was dead. My son was dead. And I should have stayed dead with them.

I died on scene, but they revived me. Every single day since, I wished they hadn't.

Recovery from having my body torn apart was long and painful. Chronic pain was just another classified issue in my mountain of problems. The scars, the meds, the migraines, the aches, all adding up to a miserable way of being alive.

Parking in the driveway, I climbed the stairs to my tiny abode. It was just as empty as I left it. The bare necessities.

Nothing—and no one else—they could take away from me.

I flopped down on the bed, cringing as my scar pulled and my knee protested. Reminders that I needed to do my stretching.

And that was how I lived my life. A stark contrast to a decade ago when I had love and we were trying to make a family.

When I was happy. When I lived.

My being could not be classified as living. More like the walking dead.

Three years of not working, of existing. Of popping pills all day long to combat the symptoms of my existence.

Every day I lived trapped in the memories. Trapped in the crash. Trapped in the aftermath.

Once an ambitious child, I knew I wanted to be a lawyer after watching shows like *Law & Order*. Later I figured out what I wanted to do and the man I wanted to be.

The end result was far off.

I hated the man I'd become. Pathetic. Broken. Angry. Fucked up beyond any and all repair.

I just wanted to close my eyes and never open them again.

It took two days for me to call Jack back, and him a half an hour to get me to agree to meet with him.

The drive to his office was easy, but with each passing mile my anxiety increased. I couldn't remember the last time I'd seen my father-in-law.

Facing any of the Holloways was difficult. They didn't blame me, even though they should have. I baited the monster and paid the highest price. Haunted by memories and an unending vendetta complete with a promise—I would never be happy again.

Death was the only way to be free.

I arrived early, because what the fuck else was I going to do with my day? That left me sitting in my car, people watching. A few minutes before noon my phone pinged with a text—Jack was running late.

There was no way I was going up. There were many people up there that knew who I was and what I was to Jack, and I hated the looks they gave me. The pity in their eyes.

With the temperature in the car heating up and me in need of a smoke, I got out and leaned against the side. I watched people come and go, moving about their day like it was nothing.

Average people that I envied.

I lit a cigarette and took a drag, then blew it out as I stared at the parking lot. Being the lunch hour, there were lots of people coming and going.

It was sunny out, warm, and as I took another pull I noticed a woman walking through the lot.

There was no particular reason why she caught my eye. She simply did. Maybe the way the sun lit up her blonde hair.

Intrigued, I stared at her. She was unassuming, skittish even.

Something inside me stirred as I stared at her. The beast inside me pulled at the chains that bound him. She called to him from across the sea of asphalt and cars.

She called to me.

Feelings I'd long forgotten awoke with an interest in her. But why?

Two men walked toward her, and I watched her change. Shoulders drew up, pace slowed, eyes down as her body went rigid as if bracing herself. From what? An attack?

It was subtle. So subtle, most wouldn't even notice.

But I did, and so did the beast.

She was nothing, no one, but she seemed a mystery I wanted to unravel.

But not.

Because nothing good came from me having interest in anything.

As soon as she passed them, her demeanor returned. Another man came by, and she relaxed.

I wanted her.

The beast wanted her. Some unknown girl, if even for just a taste.

Just a small, tiny taste.

The chains that held me in check began to loosen, and just as I was about to launch myself at her, a hand clamped down on my shoulder.

"Sorry to keep you waiting, Nathan," Jack said, breaking me from the siren's song. His brow scrunched as he looked at me. "Are you all right, son?"

I rubbed at my neck as I tried to get a grip, an understanding of what just happened to me. I'd become completely unhinged by a woman in a parking lot who never even met my gaze.

"I'm fine. Just…lost in thought." *And possibly going out of my mind.*

I glanced back at her, a woman walking with her, unaware of me or my internal struggle. Unaware of my strange behavior.

I had no clue what came over me, but it was apparent I needed to stay as far from her as I could. Which would be easy. All I had to do was stay away from Jack's office.

"What did you want to talk about?"

Jack gave me a kind smile. "We'll talk about it over lunch, but I'd like you to come work for me."

My eyes widened, my dick twitching at the thought of seeing that strange girl again.

I shook my head. "No."

Jack pursed his lips and sighed. "Come on. I'll convince you over lunch."

I wasn't so sure about that, but what harm could come from listening to his offer?

Six months later…
I sat in my car.
New car. New suit. New apartment.

New life.

Almost.

The old one still haunted me, lurked around every corner.

After almost an hour, Jack had convinced me to work for him.

No litigation.

That was key. I couldn't do litigation again.

Checking to make sure the verbiage was correct and there were no loopholes in contracts, I could do.

It had taken six months of paperwork and CLEs to get my license reinstated after having dropped off the face of the earth.

My heart raced, hands shaking as I sat there waiting for the numbers on the clock to change. Every part of me wanted to run away. But what would I be running to?

A sedan pulled up beside me and I glanced over, my eyes widening beneath my sunglasses.

It was her.

The blonde woman I'd seen months ago in the same parking lot. The enigma.

I couldn't help but stare, watching as she threw her hair up into a bun. The frown as she noticed something I wasn't able to see. Couldn't look away when she lifted her hips, dragging her skirt up to her waist. Her thumbs hooked into her pantyhose and pushed them down over her fuck perfect round ass.

Holy fuck.

My cock was as hard as steel in seconds.

Inch by inch, more smooth, pale skin was revealed.

She was so innocent looking while doing something so provocative.

Her gaze caught mine, and I couldn't stop my lip twitching up into a smirk. My dick strained against my pants as a blush spread over her skin.

I then startled when she flipped me the bird before climbing out and walking away.

My enigma was cheeky.

Fuck.

Fucking fuck.

I was fucking screwed if she was anywhere fucking near me in the building.

Holloway and Holloway had a non-fraternization policy that I had *no* interest in breaching.

There was no getting close to anyone, because there were consequences. Lives that would not be lost due to me.

After those sobering thoughts, my dick had thankfully gone down and I headed in to find Jack. Part of our arrangement was that no one who knew me was to speak a word about who I was or how Jack and I knew each other.

As fresh of a start as I could get.

The elevator was packed, and when I got off a familiar face smiled at me, then looked around before going into a neutral expression.

"It's all right, Cassie," I said to Jack's secretary.

She gave me a small smile. "Go on in. He's waiting for you."

I nodded to her. Grabbing hold of the handle, I pulled it open, which happened to be just as Jack was pushing it to step out.

"Ah, there you are."

"Am I late?"

He shook his head. "No, no, of course not. I was hoping you'd be a bit early so that I could introduce you to your partner before the announcement."

I held my arm out. "Lead the way."

We headed to the stairwell, which surprised me. He looked back at me as we ascended the stairs.

"Mary says I need to get more exercise."

My mother-in-law.

It left me wondering if working there with all the reminders was really going to work.

I tried to smile at him. Forced one, then forced it to look natural.

When we reached the landing I took in a steadying breath and brushed it all away. The accident, my family, Marconi—pushed aside.

New life.

New beginning.

All channeling the old me.

The one that got me just about anything I wanted. The one I channeled every time I went out to the bar in search of a fuck.

I stood behind Jack as he called a woman in a small office over. Noticed the way her voice seemed forced, fake like a voice used over the phone.

"I wanted to introduce you to your new roommate before the announcement was made." Jack stepped aside, and ushered me in.

Fuck.

Standing before me was none other than my enigma.

Her mouth popped open, strangely beautiful grey-green eyes wide as she stared at me. It was unnerving, because it felt like she was seeing past the façade.

Fuck.

Not her.

Anyone but her.

"This is Nathan Thorne. He'll need your guidance until he's acclimated to how we operate. Please take good care of him."

"Delilah, was it?" I smirked at her, just as I had in the parking lot, hoping for the same reaction.

Not wanting to be rude, I held out my hand. It took a beat too long for her to slip hers into mine. A stiff, formal shake. Neither wanting to give anything away.

Then we parted, Jack and I heading out.

My hands shook, heart racing, the beast inside drooling.

Fuck.

The cheeky little enigma was my office mate.

I wanted to fuck her.

Fuck her so hard bent over her desk.

Lusting after my off-limits coworker was a shitty way to start a new job. Hopefully the non-fraternization policy would be enough to keep me in check. Maybe I could make sure she stayed away.

Whatever I had to do to keep my distance.

Chapter 2

Two months after the end of Reciprocity...

The glare-down entered its fifth minute with neither of us backing down. My jaw twitched. Lila's jutted forward. A bottle of wine sat between us on the counter. The kitchen was a disaster, we both looked wrecked, and we hadn't had sex in five days.

Five fucking days.

Weeks of small spats were building, and the blowout was bound to happen at any moment. What bothered me, what hurt the most, was the reason *why* my wife and I were having such difficulties.

It wasn't because of someone coming after us, my overbearing protectiveness, or her family. No, it was *us*.

Us.

Me.

Her.

The reality of life without looking over our shoulders.

Who were Nathan and Delilah Thorne?

What did they like? What did they do in their spare time? Hobbies?

The only hobby I had was fucking her, and that wasn't happening lately because one or both of us was constantly angry at the other for sometimes unknown, irrational reasons.

Sex was no longer providing the way to connect.

There was a glitch in our system. We needed a reboot.

All I wanted to do was take her over my lap, spank the shit out of her for being difficult, then shove my cock in her. Problem being that it wouldn't solve anything, and she wasn't in the frame of mind to relent to my dominance. My Honeybear was a hard-headed, strong-willed fighter. I'd be lucky if I came out with my cock still attached.

She wasn't fucking giving in.

Giving in to what was the new question. To me? I wasn't sure.

It had been so many days, I couldn't remember what we were even fighting about. I'm sure she did, though, and I would be a dead man for not knowing.

The phone in my pocket chirped, and her eyes narrowed. Without batting at eye, I pulled the phone out and accepted the call.

"Thorne."

"Whoa. You okay?"

I clenched my jaw and took note of how Lila's knuckles were white from her grip on the edge of the counter. "Fine, Drew. What's up?"

"I know it's late, but I've got a hearing in the morning and I just received information on a pending case against my client that impacts his financials. I hate to ask, man, but since you've become the lawsuit guru, I could really use your help. I've been staring at it so long it's looking like gibberish."

Lila pushed away from the counter, still staring at me as she backed up, then turned and walked out of the room.

Since my night wasn't bound to improve... "I'll be there in twenty."

I didn't even wait for a response before hanging up. With Lila banging around somewhere in the bedroom, I took a moment to try to cool off. Tempers were out of control, and my whole body radiated with so many powerful emotions that I was actually afraid of what I might do.

My personal trainer, Jared, had to cancel on me that day, and I greatly needed that outlet.

I took a deep breath and headed to the entry. "I have to go to—"

"I know! I heard. Bye." Lila cut me off.

The urge to punch the wall was strong.

I made sure to slam the door as hard as I could on my way out, just to make her jump, even though I wouldn't see it. My anger wasn't enough to stop my compulsive locking of the door before I stomped down the hall to the elevator. Angry or not, protecting Lila, even in such a small fashion, was mandatory to my nature.

The ride to the office gave me time to think, though no answers to any of my questions came. I was able to decompress a little, but it wasn't enough.

Every cell in my body shook. A ticking time bomb, ready to explode—a feeling so extreme I'd forgotten how overwhelming it was. Over a year ago, it was a normal reaction Lila incited in me, but now it was for different reasons while still related to her.

At almost eight in the evening, there was still half a dozen cars in the parking lot, including Owen's—months later Jack still had Lila on a restricted forty-hour work week.

An elevator ride and a quiet walk down the hall led me to one of the only lights shining from the open doors. I tapped on the door, and Drew's blond head popped up.

"Hey, Nate," he said as he started to smile, then frowned. "Is everything okay?"

I shook my head and leaned on the door frame. "No."

"What's going on?"

I let out a harsh sigh as I fell into the chair in front of his desk. "Vincent Marconi is dead and his organization is crumbling. Adam is in jail. Life should be rainbows and fucking sunshine, but my marriage is blowing up."

His brow scrunched up. "Wait…what? You should be kicking back and enjoying life after everything you've been through."

I leaned forward and ran my hands over my face. "Should, but I think that's part of the problem. I don't think we know how to do that."

"Well, you've been through a lot. Did you really think everything would be perfect with Marconi dead? It's been so long for both of you. Do you even know how to *live*?"

I shook my head. "I don't think we do." I blew out a breath and looked back up at him. "So, what's your hang-up?"

It didn't take long to help Drew with his problem. Most of it was due to a combination of staring at it for too long and the panic of new information. A fresh set of eyes, and problem solved. However, two hours had managed to pass since I left home.

Stopping at a light on the way home a glint of light caught my eye, my gaze moving to it. The platinum wedding band on my left hand was shining in the streetlight. To me, it was a symbol of rebirth and a love for a woman who was part of my soul.

Why couldn't I figure out how to fix us?

I always knew what she needed. Always so in tune with her.

After the trial, after Vincent's death, life was finally clearing up. Once Tom was out of the hospital, his team hit the Marconi hard with legal troubles.

But when the dust settled, so did reality and a confusion neither of us was expecting.

We didn't know what to do or who we were.

So much time had been spent running, but what did you do when the treadmill stopped?

It was nearly midnight when I returned home. With each floor that ticked by in the elevator, another expectation of what awaited me passed through my mind. The fighting was tiring, draining, and I didn't want any more of it tonight. I just wanted to go to bed, curled up with my wife.

I took a deep breath and slowly let it out as I opened the door.

Silence greeted me, but our condo was still half lit. The kitchen lights were on as well as a lamp in the living room.

After hanging up my coat, I began popping the buttons of my shirt as I made my way to the bedroom. Low murmuring came from the television, but the bed was empty.

"Lila?" I called out.

Small speckles on the carpet caught my eye from the glow of the open ensuite door. The dark red color sent a spike of panic through me as I rushed forward, my heart hammering in my constricting chest. The door bounced off the stopper as my eyes snapped around to each new smear of red.

"Lila?"

No. Not now. There was no reason now. We didn't matter any longer. Not to anyone. So why? Where?

I raced back out to the living room searching for any evidence, any clue, as to what happened, but everywhere I looked was normal. No signs of a struggle anywhere.

The illumination at the end of the hall drew me in. Slow, careful steps. Quiet. I pushed on the door, frantically looking around for anyone.

Lila was there, sitting at her desk, head lying on top of her folded arms. As I walked to her I noticed her hand was bandaged. Reaching out, I pushed a few strands from her face.

"Baby?"

She grunted, her eyes fluttering open before closing again, then settled back down.

I smirked and leaned over, drawing her up and into my arms. She didn't wake, but her hands did clutch onto my shirt and she nuzzled into my neck.

Having her in my arms was calming. Her body against mine provided a small snippet of that connection we've been missing.

The grip she had on me refused to release as I laid her down. I reached out and swept the hair from her face. "It's okay, baby. I'm home."

Her fingers relaxed, slipping down to the bed.

After covering her with the blanket, I walked into the kitchen to get some supplies to clean up the trail of splattered blood. It started in the closet, the first drops, along with the offending item—a cardboard box. I stared down at it and shook my head. Such an innocuous, simple-looking item. Harmless.

The panic it incited was laughable as it sat there with its flaps at odd angles.

After cleaning up, I pulled my clothes off and climbed into bed. There, I did what I always did, and pulled her to me—chest to back. The sweet smell of her hair calmed me, along with each slow, steady breath.

The next morning I woke up to the sound of my alarm. I slammed my hand down and rubbed my eyes. I stretched out beside me, but the bed was empty. She wasn't there. However, the shower was running, thus halting the rising panic attack.

I sat up and swung my legs over the edge of the bed. My knee throbbed, as did my head, threatening to turn into a violent migraine. Add in the ache in my ribs and wrist, and I knew the weather was going to be rain filled. Probably with thunderstorms.

Limping my way into the bathroom, I entered just as Lila opened the shower door. She jumped in surprise, probably shocked from my zombie-like walking and tired eyes.

I reached out for her and she stepped back, but I caught her wrist and pulled it toward me. Looking down, I inspected the cut. Thankfully, it seemed to have sealed itself, but it was a bit larger than I thought and by her hiss, quite tender.

My gaze ran up her arm, cringing inside when the white circle patch of skin on her shoulder came into view. There was no time I could ever imagine the site of her wound from Marconi's bullet wouldn't cause some violent reaction within me.

"Stitches?"

She shook her head. "I think it'll be fine."

I pulled off my underwear and switched places with her, hating the gap as she squeezed by.

Hating each second of walking on eggshells.

Hating the silence.

Hating how much I just wanted to touch her, but had to stop myself.

Hating how we were both mad, but still madly in love.

Because even with all the crap of the prior weeks, I remained completely and totally in love with her. A few weeks of fighting could never and would never be enough to shake that.

When I stepped out a few minutes later and a whole lot cleaner, Lila stood at the sink, blow-dryer on full blast, her hand wrapped up again in gauze. Toweling off, I walked back into the bedroom in search of what suit to wear.

In the closet hung three suits.

Three.

I tilted my head back and blew out, my jaw jutting forward.

"Lila!"

The blow-dryer was still going, and I knew she couldn't hear me, so I went back to the bathroom.

"Lila!"

I caught her gaze in the mirror and her thumb flipped the switch, the noise level dropping and reminding me how much my head was thumping.

"Did you pick up the dry cleaning?"

Her brow scrunched and she shook her head. "It's your week."

"I dropped them off this week. You were supposed to." Our alternating schedule usually worked out without issue, but the three suits hanging in my closet meant we were more than one week out.

"I picked them up last week. On Thursday when you were with Jared."

"Last Thursday you went out with Caroline."

She shook her head. "Whatever. It's not that big of a deal. We'll pick it up tonight."

"If we have any clothes for work."

She crossed her arms in front of her and leaned her hip against the counter. "What? It's my fault?"

"Yes. Clothes have been dropped off, but not picked up. Two weeks' worth."

"We can pick them up after work."

"We have to, otherwise neither of us will have enough clothes for work to get through next week."

"And you didn't pick them up last week, or we wouldn't have two weeks' worth."

I turned, my head shaking back and forth, teeth mashing as I returned to the closet to pick from the laundry leftovers. The whole ordeal left me wondering how we both managed to not notice our dwindling attire.

Dark grey suit was the winner. Luckily, all of my suits were fairly new, purchased right before I started and all close in style.

After getting dressed and ready, I went to the kitchen for some breakfast.

Even after a shower and moving around, everything still hurt.

Thump.

Thump.

Thump.

Incessant and going along with the tick in my eye as I stared at the gallon of milk sitting on the counter—a leftover ingredient of dinner.

"Fuck."

"What?" Lila asked, entering behind me.

I twisted the top off the container and moved to the sink, pouring over half a gallon down the drain.

"What are you doing?"

"You left it out last night."

"*I* did?"

It was that tone. The one that had become like nails on a chalkboard and the telltale ding of the next round.

"You made the alfredo sauce. Now there's no milk for breakfast."

Her gaze narrowed, fists clenched at her side. I tried not to zoom in on the gauze wrapped around her hand, on remembering my panic the night before, but it flooded me. I hated seeing her in any kind of pain, yet every day we were dishing it out at each other, and I couldn't stand it.

Something was wrong with her emotionally—and me—but I couldn't help. That was where the gap between us came in, growing wider every day as we pushed each other away.

"What the fuck is your problem this morning?"

I rinsed out the container and turned, glaring at her. "What isn't?" *Here we fucking go.* "Do I need to start back in with the lack of clothing?"

She threw up her arms in the air. "I can't believe you're still harping on that. We can pick up the dry cleaning on the way in." She reached for her purse. "Let's go."

"Why the hurry?"

"If we have to make an extra stop, we need the extra time." There was annoyance in her tone.

"Not trying to get in early?"

What the fuck am I doing?

Good question. Testy, uncontrollable anger and frustration for no reason. No logical reason, at least. "You're wearing your flirty skirt today. Didn't know if that was for your intern."

Her jaw dropped open as she stared at me and shook her head. "We've already had the discussion about the lack of clothing. Besides, I wear this to work all the time and you quite like it."

She was trying to defuse me, and that just amped me up more.

"Me and every other guy."

Her hand slammed down on the counter. "Fucking stop! Being stupid jealous is not helping things."

"Stupid jealous?" I asked through gritted teeth.

Tears filled her eyes, her body so tense she was shaking. "Yes. It's not sexy jealousy, it's just another fucking excuse to incite a fight."

She was right. I wasn't really jealous of Chris, her intern. Anger clawed at the one thing I desperately wanted, and I was lashing out with any excuse.

"Fuck!" I grabbed hold of the nearest thing and flung it at the wall. The wine glass shattered and landed in hundreds of pieces on the floor.

"I can fucking do that, too," she said, "but it doesn't fucking change anything. We're still two fucked-up people pissed at each other."

My jaw clenched, and I stared at the spot on the cabinet the glass had hit. "I don't want to be pissed. I'm fucking tired of this shit."

She was silent for a minute, then her voice came out in a small whisper I could barely hear. "Me too."

I wanted to call her Honeybear. To pull her into my arms. To fuck the sense out of both of us.

To feel anything but the void between us.

An hour later we survived a silent drive to the office and equally silent ride up the elevator. We walked beside each other, my fingers itching to grab her hand with every step.

Why did shit have to be so complicated?

"Lunch?" she asked as we stopped in front of her office door.

I nodded, my jaw clenching and unclenching. "Somewhere close. We have Darren tonight."

"I know." It was an involuntary snap back. I could tell by the way her eyes widened, then shifted to the floor as her shoulders tensed, drawing up.

It was a reaction that didn't happen often, but killed me when it did. Still stuck with a fear she might never shake. Fear that her talking back would earn a hit. The last thing I ever wanted was for her to be afraid of me.

I reached out for her arm. The simple touch of my fingers releasing the tension, and she stepped forward. A small kiss to her forehead. A silent "I love you."

"I'll see you later."

She nodded and moved to her desk. I couldn't help but watch.

When she looked up and our eyes met, the same sadness laced in anger I felt in myself stared back. Turning, I headed down the hall to my office.

Therapy had to help us, because I didn't think I could stand much more of the abyss.

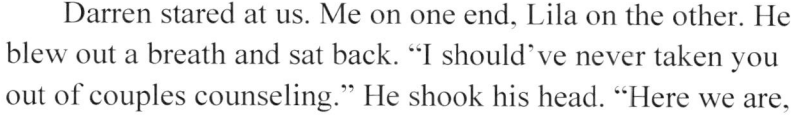

Darren stared at us. Me on one end, Lila on the other. He blew out a breath and sat back. "I should've never taken you out of couples counseling." He shook his head. "Here we are, a month back into it, and it appears that things are only getting worse."

We both remained silent, both stewing and not knowing what to say.

"Are you going to tell me what's going on, or do I have to play twenty questions?"

Again, silence.

"Okay, twenty questions it is." He cleared his throat, glanced down at his notebook, then between us. "Lila, how's your shoulder?"

Her mouth dropped open, then closed. "Fine."

I shook my head.

"Nathan, do you disagree?"

I turned to her. "You're not fine."

Her jaw jutted forward. "And how do you know?"

The blood in my veins ticked, heating as it pumped viciously through me. "Who's always around you? Who watches you? Sees you struggle to get dressed? Do chores? Even drive?"

"Well, maybe that's the problem."

I leaned back, the blood that was fire turning ice cold. "Which is it, Lila? I'm around too much or not enough?"

Her brow scrunched up and her arms knotted tighter.

"Lila, what's wrong?" Darren asked, staring her down. She didn't budge, just stared at the ground. "Can you find words for what you feel?"

"Feel?" Her voice was barely a whisper, a tear slipping from her eyes. "I feel the overwhelming panic. The fear and pain... I see the gun lined up, stare down the barrel, and wait."

Darren perked up at her last word. "Are you still waiting?"

There was a pause. "Yes," she said, the word breaking.

A sound I couldn't even identify tore from my chest.

Arms holding me back. Vincent standing over her. Blood pouring from her.

Helpless.

Unable to protect the one thing I swore I'd die to protect.

Watching him take my wife from me. Again.

I rolled off the couch into a standing position, unable to take the tightness growing in my chest. Pacing began as I tried to calm myself.

Darren shot me a glance, then turned back to Lila. "How often do you think about it?"

"All the time," she whispered.

"You've mentioned this to me in passing in our private sessions. Have you ever mentioned it to Nathan before?"

I looked over to her. It was the first I'd heard of it, but why?

"No."

"And why is that?"

She tucked her head in even closer to her chest. "Because I don't want to remind him."

"Do you think he's forgotten?"

Not for a second.

She shook her head.

"Do you think he goes through the same thing?"

She stayed unmoving.

My hands fisted and relaxed in a pulsing beat that match the tensing of my muscles as I stared at her.

"Nathan, why are you so agitated?" Darren asked, but I was certain he knew the answer. He just wanted me to say it out loud.

"Do you have *any* idea what that did to me?" I growled through clenched teeth. "To watch him shoot you, then put a fucking gun to your head?"

The last part came out as a yell, making her shrink back. She refused to look at me. "I know it was hard."

I let out a harsh grunt. "Hard doesn't even fucking cover it! I died in those seconds. I wanted that bullet lined up to my head because I can't… I can't…" The words caught in my throat. A vice wrapped around my chest, and I felt tears sliding down my face. Her hand slid across the open space between us, but I returned to pacing the floor. "You're waiting to die, and I'm dying in the wait."

"Exactly."

I stopped and turned to Darren. "What the fuck does that mean?"

"What you said. It's why you're off. You may not be hunted anymore, but you're both haunted." He looked between us, and by his expression, it seemed he had it all figured out, like always. "You're mad, because Lila gave up. She accepted what was about to happen, while you fight against it still."

"How could I not? There was no way out. I made peace with it. And then I was still alive and we were okay, but I feel like we are dead and this is purgatory."

I kneeled down in front of her, my hands resting on the tops of her thighs. "We're not dead. We're alive. No one is coming for us."

"How do you know?" she asked, her brow scrunched, bottom lip quivering.

"I don't," I said, taking her hands in mine, "but I don't think they care now that Vincent is dead. It was *his* vendetta. And we can't live a life waiting for them to come back."

Her bottom lip trembled. "I don't know how to shake this."

I placed a light kiss on her fingers. "The same way we do everything—together."

"He's right."

We both looked to Darren. "The two of you are strongest together. I'm just your mediator. Forcing you to voice the thoughts that haunt you."

I reached out and cupped her cheek. Something inside clicked back into place when she leaned into me. Those beautiful eyes of hers met mine, and for the first time in weeks, truly connected.

"I'm scared."

"I know, Honeybear, but I'm here. I'm always right beside you."

Where I would always be for the rest of our lives.

The atmosphere in the car was lighter on the way home than it had been on the way to see Darren. Finally, it seemed peace was settling back in.

"How's your work husband doing?" I asked, trying to keep the lighter atmosphere close.

"Work husband?"

"Yeah. Owen."

She shook her head. "You know, my actual, living, breathing husband works for the same employer with his office just down the hall, so technically he's my work husband."

I chuckled. "While that may be true, working so close to you, there is a relationship between you two."

"Really?"

I nodded, my foot hitting the gas as the light changed. "Yes. He knows how you like your coffee, can tell when you aren't feeling well."

"He's a sweet guy." Her lips spread into a smile. "His girlfriend is lucky. Or is this your way of telling me you're jealous?"

My lip twitched, and I shrugged. "Maybe."

"Maybe?"

"A little," I grumbled. I was a jealous ass when it came to my wife. She was *mine*.

"Why?"

"First off, because you're mine, but also because I miss having our desks touching."

She smiled at me. "I miss you too. Besides, I get jealous as well. I mean, it's not like the Boob Squad has disappeared. They're still always around and flirting with you."

"Jennifer's gone. Fired. Remember?" I sure did. Lila rode me so hard in my office that day.

The corners of her mouth turned down as a disgusted look covered her face. "God, she was the worst."

"And it hasn't been nearly as bad since we got married."

"Not now that their ringleader is jobless."

There was a shift in the car and that sweet, familiar heat that moved between us, the one I missed so very much, filled the air, crackling between us, almost tangible.

My fingers clenched around the steering wheel as my cock hardened. My tongue swiped across my lips, and I glanced to Lila. Her cheeks were flushed, hands clenched together, thighs rubbing against each other.

I reached out and grabbed onto her thigh, causing her to gasp, her hips rising off the seat.

Days without each other's touch left us with an intense physical reaction. So much so that I wasn't sure I'd be able to make it to the parking lot, up the elevator, and inside our home.

The hard cock in my pants was in control, slamming my foot on the gas, propelling us faster down the highway.

I wanted her against the wall, against the one I'd taken out so many of my feelings for her.

"Nathan..." The breathy whisper of my name from her lips made me groan.

The second we were in a parking spot, I turned the car off and jumped out. Grabbing on to her hand, I practically dragged her inside.

"Hi, Mike," Lila said, giving the guard a wave as we ran past.

In the elevator bay, I pressed the button more times than needed. I knew it wouldn't help get the elevator any faster, but if I didn't do it, I was going to do X-rated things to my wife in the lobby.

The elevator arrived, and the second we were on I shoved her against the wall. I leaned down and kissed her, making sure to push my tongue into her mouth. To taste her, to let her know how much I wanted her.

When we broke apart, she let out a small giggle—a sound that had only appeared in the last year. Cheeks pink, lips swollen, and the sexiest little smile let me know my vixen was just as ready as I was.

"Is there something you want, Mr. Thorne?"

I reached out and pressed the button for our floor before running my hand up her thigh, under her skirt. I cupped her pussy, pressing my fingers in, making her squirm against me.

"Well, Mrs. Thorne, I want this pussy. It's been way too long."

Her thighs parted and she grabbed onto my shirt, pulling me closer. "What is it that you want to do?"

A smirk grew on my face as I pulled her panties aside, my thumb finding her clit, making her jump. "I want to stick my cock in my pussy and fuck it until the insides are painted white. I want you begging like a whore for more."

"Fuck."

The second the doors slid open I was dragging her down the hall, fumbling with the keys as I located the one for the door.

Six days since I'd been inside my wife.

Six days since I'd gotten off.

As soon as the door was open, she walked through and I followed, shutting and locking the door behind me.

I turned and cupped her face in my hands, my lips pressing against hers as I walked her back against the wall. Our teeth clattered together when she did.

Moving down, I trailed kisses down her neck, her hands working my belt open as I reached down to pull her skirt up. When it was bunched around her waist, I grabbed under her thighs and lifted her.

"I wasn't done." Her whimper went straight to my cock that she was trying to get to.

I shook my head. "Don't worry." I reached between us and pulled my dick out before sliding her panties aside.

The head of my cock pressed against her slit before sliding into her wet pussy. A guttural moan slipped out of both of us, and I leaned forward, resting my forehead on hers.

That was it. The missing piece. The connection I'd been itching for.

Our eyes locked as I pulled out and pushed back in, and it felt like every piece of me was finally back in place.

We were back in place.

I trailed one hand up her thigh as I pressed her against the wall.

"I'm alive. You're alive." I grabbed onto her abdomen, flexing my fingers. "And I'm going to fuck life into here."

"Fuck!"

I pulled out and slammed my hips forward. "I think it's about time my little cock slut gave me a baby. Then you'll know you're alive, and we're okay, and everything will be okay."

Her pussy tightened around me, a stuttered curse blown from her breath. "Yes."

It wasn't going to be a marathon. I'd save that for after. I was in a sprint.

Cries of pleasure echoed off the walls as I dug in, pounding into her. It was too much. Too built up.

"I can't..." I trailed off, unable to form words as I attempted to hold back, my whole body shaking.

"Come in me."

All of my muscles tensed, come blasting from my cock. I shook in violent spasms as I emptied inside her.

Strength left me, breath harsh, the last twitches pushing out the final drops.

We slid down to the floor, my head resting on her shoulder. Her fingers combed through my hair as I came down from one of the most intense orgasms of my life.

Blue balls was no fucking joke. My balls hurt after a week of neglect.

"This isn't going to be easy," I said, placing a kiss on her shoulder.

Her breath was just as harsh as mine. "It never is."

"But we'll get past this as we have everything else—together."

She nodded against me. "Together."

Chapter 3

Year One...

After a six-month search, Lila and I found a home in Carmel—land of the roundabouts—and had settled in to suburban living. With the lives we'd led, it was quite an adjustment. Being neighborly was a foreign concept for Lila, leaving some of our neighbors a little put off.

She wasn't the stereotypical suburban housewife like many of the nearby residents.

There was a good chance we would never fit in well, but it didn't bother me. She was all I needed.

We had a beautiful lot overlooking a small lake. It made for wonderful nights sitting on the deck, watching the sun set.

I stared at her, my eyes wide in surprise at her sudden burst of anger. My wife was livid—pissed beyond belief at me—and I had no idea why. Her face resembled the same shade of red as the Twizzler dangling out of my mouth. I held up my hands in surrender, never having seen the she-devil before me, and I had no idea how to handle her.

"Why?" Her hands were balled into fists at her sides, shaking.

Why, what? I asked internally, afraid to voice the words and the reaction they would incite.

Lila was beautiful in pregnancy, but at times she turned into someone I didn't know. I'd heard about the behavior from others, but hardly experienced it myself as Grace never made it to the she-beast stage.

I really needed to stop calling her she-beast in my head. I was bound to slip one day and then she'd kill me.

I chewed at the Twizzler, buying some more time. The shrill noise that escaped her as her face screwed up made me jump. She stomped forward and I backed up, but instead of swiping at me with her claws, she grabbed the package of red, chewy goodness. Tears welled in her eyes as she looked at the half-eaten package, then back at me. Bewildered, I stared at the hurt on her face before she turned and headed toward the back porch. The door slammed behind her, shaking the frame.

I flipped the Twizzler between my teeth and looked down at it. "Huh." Mental note—anything you eat for the next month *must* be from a hidden stash.

I'd come in to get us some drinks and, in the process of making them, chewed on a pack of candy sitting on the counter. After the ice cream debacle the week before, I thought I understood, but it was obvious I knew nothing.

I licked my lips. At least the ice cream fiasco had a happy ending. Fuck. I'd never felt her pussy squeeze my cock so hard. It would also be a scene I'd never forget—eight-months-pregnant wife riding me while eating a pint of Ben & Jerry's.

Pregnant woman really could be scary as fuck.

A few days later we found ourselves at the courthouse, in a situation that brought back memories from two years prior. A situation I had strong objections of subjecting my very pregnant wife to.

"Why are we here?" Lila's jaw was locked just as tight as her hand was around mine, the other rubbing her belly.

"Because they need to see what kind of monster he is so they can keep him locked up longer."

I really didn't like the stress the whole situation was putting on her, but it was a necessity. Adam had attacked a guard, and Lila had been called back in as a character witness against him. My only hope was that we could get it over and done with before it pushed Lila into an early delivery. There were still four weeks before our little girl was due.

Down the hall, near the courtroom doors, stood Lawrence. "Are you ready?"

Lila shook her head, tears welling up in her eyes. "I thought I was done with this, with *him*. With reliving all that…" Her gaze snapped to Lawrence. "Is *he* here?"

"Your father?" he asked.

Fuck! How could I have not even thought of that?

Lawrence shook his head. "He won't be here, don't worry. His character is just as bad, so there was no way Adam's attorney wanted him on the stand."

She let out a sigh of relief and continued to rub her hand over her belly.

"That and the restraining order," I reminded her.

He nodded. "That, too."

We walked in and took our seats behind Lawrence. Lila's hand shook in mine, and I was thankful that this time we wouldn't be separated.

A door in the back swung open, and out stepped two guards with a chained-up, orange-clad Adam. Even after over a year in jail he was as obstinate as ever, pulling against the cuffs and the officer who tried to pull him along when he slowed his pace.

When he looked up, his dark eyes searched out and immediately landed on us—on Lila. Her head was down in a refusal to look at him, to be subjected to the nasty vibes he was letting off.

My leg began to bounce, the stress she was under eating me up. Agitation fueled the anger I was trying to stifle in order to be strong for her, to be the foundation she so desperately needed. Because Adam was the only person to shake her to the core, and I wanted nothing more in that moment than his blood on my hands.

I kissed her temple and she relaxed a bit, her head rising as the screeching of the chairs echoed around the room. Soon, the judge came in and the proceedings began.

Opening statements, the charges against him—assault of a guard—and then it was time.

I stood, blocking her from his view as she walked to the aisle. With a kiss to her hand, I let her go, wishing I could block her from him the entire time.

As soon as she was away, I turned to Adam. As she passed by he lifted his head to watch her, probably to glare at her, but instead his eyes widened, focused on the large curve of her belly. A split second later he was on his feet, chair pushed back.

"A baby?" A snarl formed on his lips, and he lunged forward. "Fucking slut! I'll fucking tear it out of you, whore!"

I ran forward, pulling her into my arms and spinning her around, protecting my family as his lawyer attempted to hold him back. The bailiffs made it before Adam trampled the scared man, and threw Adam to the ground.

"I'll kill you! I'll fucking kill you and that thing in you!"

Something about Lila always set him off. The possession he felt about her was on a destructive level, his obsession dangerous. The closest I could come up with was a petulant child throwing a tantrum that his toy was taken away.

That is what she did—took herself away. She had power and strength despite all he'd done, and he resented her for that. Always meant to be his plaything, punished whenever he wanted, destroyed when he was done.

He never got the chance to break her the way he wanted, and to see that another man took her, bred her, only solidified the loss.

Her sobs pulled my attention away from the deranged man on the floor and back to her. I pulled her closer and held her tight.

"Shh, Honeybear, I've got you. He's not getting anywhere near you. Not now, not ever."

"Enough!" the judged yelled. "Bailiff, get him out of my courtroom!"

The bailiffs nodded and pulled him to his feet. Adam continued to lunge toward Lila, snarling and screaming.

"Mrs. Thorne, please take a seat."

We made our way back to the gallery and sat down. The judge was beyond livid.

"Mr. Ackerson, please inform your client that he is in contempt of court."

"Your honor—"

"Too late. The behavior he has shown here today indicates he has no true knowledge that what he has done is wrong. In fact, he threatened the life of a witness, a punishable offense, and charges will be brought against him. I'm not entirely sure any amount of time will tone down the obvious bloodthirst he has for her." He turned to us. "Mrs. Thorne, I've seen what I need to, and there will be no reason for you to return for this offense. I wish you a safe delivery." He turned back to Adam's lawyer. "As for you, Mr. Ackerson, we will set a new date to see your client again with the hopes that he can restrain himself from another outburst."

By the fidgeting of his hands and quick nodding, I could tell Adam's lawyer was shaken. Probably court appointed as he wasn't the same from the trial. He had no idea what he was in for.

"What does this mean?" I asked Lawrence as soon as we were in the hall.

"Well, I'll file the charges for the threat and that should pad his sentence some, or at least make the possibility of early release non-existent. Add that to the assault of the guard, and we're looking at the possibility of another eight years to his sentence." He smiled, seeming as happy with the outcome as I was.

"Thank you, Lawrence," Lila said, holding out her hand.

He smiled at her and shook her hand. "Good luck in your delivery."

"Thank you."

Lawrence started to walk away, but I stopped him. "Not to sound like an ass, but I hope we never have to see you again."

He smirked and nodded, understanding my meaning and giving a wave as he headed off.

Wrapping my arm around Lila's shoulders, we turned to walk in the other direction. I tilted my head and kissed her hair.

"What does Mommy want for lunch?"

She seemed to perk up at the idea of food. "Samosas and tacos."

I pursed my lips and nodded. "Right." Whatever my babies wanted.

When we arrived home after stopping at two places for lunch, I had Lila relax on the couch while I made her some tea. Once done, I grabbed the TV remote and sat next to her. She was staring down at her belly, and I followed her gaze.

There was a small bump on top of her rather large baby bump. Just as I was about to say something, it moved, drawing along her stomach, then away.

"Was that the baby?"

"Yes, unless there is an alien inside me."

She pulled up her shirt, and we both stared transfixed as a hand or foot popped up, stretching against Lila's skin. I placed my hand on her stomach, and a jolt pulsed through me as our baby bumped me.

"She's never been this active before."

"Probably senses your stress," I said, running my hand around.

"Maybe the fried ice cream, too."

Another kick, maybe a punch.

My baby.

Pride pumped through me.

I marked Lila as mine. Branded her.

Fucking poured my come into her, filled her up until she was good and bred.

My DNA mixed with hers.

I leaned down and pressed my lips to her stomach. "It's almost time, Anna. Then we finally get to meet you."

It was hard to believe we were so close. That we would be parents.

Anna was the perfect name choice. Lila's mother was the only one to show her love until she was a late teenager, and she was taken from her way too soon.

"I love you," she said, staring into my eyes.

I smiled and pressed my lips to hers. "Forever."

Chapter 4

Year Two...

"Oh my God, look how adorable you are!" Caroline held Anna high up in the air, then brought her little baby belly to her mouth and blew on it, making Anna squeal in delight.

Our little bundle arrived without issue, just an exhausting delivery, with my hair and Lila's eyes. At nine months old, she was already exhibiting signs of the rambunctious child she would grow into.

Lila smiled at them. "You say that every time you see her."

"Can't blame her. She got her looks from her mom."

I turned in my seat. "Drew, are you saying I've got an ugly mug?"

He gave a snort and shook his head. "You still have women in the office chasing your ass. So, no. Just saying Lila is beautiful."

I pointed my finger at him. "Hey, that's my wife."

Lila rolled her eyes and swatted my arm before going over to Drew and giving him a hug.

"Thanks, Drew, I needed that."

"Needed that? Is Nate falling down on the job?" He gave me a mock glare, and I flipped him off.

She shook her head, and I couldn't help but wait less than patiently for her response.

"Not in the least, but sometimes it's just nice to hear from someone other than my husband. He's kind of biased."

I narrowed my gaze on her. "What was that?"

She sat down on my lap and rubbed her hand against my chest. "Everyone has a little vanity in them. Besides, reassurance is good when you're married to the one of the most desired men in the office."

"Wait, one of? I'm not most eligible anymore?" I asked, half stunned, half joking.

"Getting married and having a kid knocked you down. Plus the two interns right now." Caroline waved her hand in front of her face. "They've got me wanting to cougar all over them."

I let out a laugh. "Those are just fantasies now, married lady."

Caroline held out her hand and sighed with the biggest smile on her face as she stared down at her wedding set.

It was out of the blue, a whim. A trip to the Hamilton County courthouse to file some paperwork with Ian along for lunch turned into an impromptu marriage.

"Want to help me get her dressed?" Lila asked Caroline.

She nodded and stood, cradling Anna on her hip.

Drew and I stood as well, following them up.

"Where's Dana?" I asked him as we walked down the hall.

"She's helping her sister with a garage sale."

"How's the ring shopping going?" Caroline asked as we all stepped into Anna's room.

Drew smiled. He'd been dating Dana for over two years and had spent the last months shopping for the perfect engagement ring. "It's good. I think I've finally narrowed it down."

"I want to see them, don't forget," Caroline said, locking eyes with him until he nodded in agreement. "You went for the white one?" Caroline pointed to the dresser.

Fuck.

I looked over at Lila, who was staring at me.

At the pause, Caroline glanced between us. "Oh, this I gotta hear."

"I'll start," I said, clearing my throat and ready to dive in to the ridiculousness of the dresser debacle. "We went to IKEA to get the dresser in the brownish grey color, only to discover it had been discontinued in the dressers." I blew out a breath and pursed my lips. "As we looked at the other colors, the whitewash seemed like the one to go with."

Lila took over. "But then I started thinking about the room and the off-white walls and asked him what he thought of the black one when he interrupted me with, 'So, we're getting the whitewash.'" Lila threw her hands up.

Caroline smiled and shook her head. "You got the whitewash."

Lila continued. "And once it was together and we put it in here and saw how hideous it looked against the off-white wall, he goes 'I'm almost thinking the black one would have been better.'"

"She almost strangled me," I said with a laugh. "But in my defense, if she would have said she wanted the black, we would have gotten it. I then asked if she wanted to take it back."

"There was no way." Lila shook her head. "We'd spent over an hour putting the damn thing together. I was not about to do it all again."

Caroline's head tilted back with laughter. "Oh my God. That is hysterical."

"You have that to look forward to."

She shook her head. "No, because I won't let Ian dictate the color. The man has no style sense."

Ah, the compromises of marriage.

I pulled my wife closer and kissed the top of her head.

If that was the worst of our arguments, things were going to be just fine.

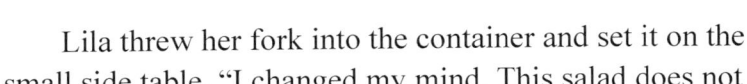

Lila threw her fork into the container and set it on the small side table. "I changed my mind. This salad does not look appetizing at all."

Eating in my office had become a once-a-week or more date. A small snippet of time where it was just me and my Honeybear.

"Told you to get the chicken sandwich."

She rolled her eyes as she took a bite of the piece of garlic bread that came with it. "I'm still trying to lose baby weight."

"Baby, there is no weight you need to lose." And I was damn serious. The ten or fifteen pounds she had on her turned me on. Her curves were accentuated, making her a damn goddess in my eyes.

She gave me a shy smile and picked up her tea. I took another bite of my sandwich, watching as she squinted, her head tilting and staring at it as she shook it.

"What are you doing?" I asked, quirking my brow at her strange behavior.

She squinted more as she held the bottle up. "There's something weird in my tea."

I took the bottle from her and turned it in the light. My lip quirked as I tried to hold some laughter in. "Reminds me of that time I helped you with your coffee."

"What are you…oh." She stared at it. "Oh my God, there's jizz in my tea?"

"It wasn't me this time." I chuckled.

"It can't really be, can it?"

I shrugged. "I can only tell you what it looks like to me."

She put the tea down, her lips turning down into a disgusted face. "Gross."

"You didn't mind it so much when I did it." I winked at her.

"Because that was yours. I got it right from the source." She reached out and grabbed hold of my cock, making me choke on my sandwich before she let go.

I coughed and took a sip of water. "Baby, if you keep talking like that and touching my dick, we're going to have a repeat right here, right now."

She turned, her eyebrow quirked and one corner of her lips pulled up into a smirk. My limp dick twitched in my pants and began to fill them. I reached down and adjusted my slacks, giving it a little more room. It was an action she stared at with great interest that only made my dick harden that much faster.

Two fucking days since I last fucked her, and my dick was ready in less than a minute.

She stood and reached behind her, my dick twitching almost in time with each click of her zipper as it moved down. Glued to the sight of it shifting before she gave it a little tug to become a pile on the floor. Her thumbs hooked into her panties and I licked my lips, watching them slide down her smooth legs, letting me see the pussy I loved so much.

"How much time do we have?" My sandwich was long forgotten, abandoned on the side table.

She stepped forward and straddled my legs. "Enough time for a fuck."

"Damn, I love it when you say fuck." I worked open my belt, then my slacks.

A quick shuffle, just enough to get my cock out, before she was straddling me. Fucking mind-wiping bliss as I watched my hungry pussy swallow my cock. I reached out, my hands framing her hips.

"Best fucking sight," I groaned, hips flexing as she moved up and down.

Leaning forward, she placed her hand next to my head on the back of the chair. Her lips were parted, eyes clouded.

I leaned my head back and reached for her, my tongue sliding across her open mouth, coaxing her down just enough for me to devour her mouth.

Soft whimpers flowed from her into me as I growled back in return. My fingers dug into her hips, changing the pace.

No longer fucking me. I was fucking her.

"You can ride my come from me soft and slow later. I'll be fucking you now."

Forced to hold on, I moved her like a rag doll along my shaft as I pulled her down as my hips slammed up. As much as she tried to hold them in, her moans were growing in volume while her pussy tightened around me. The smacking of our bodies colliding echoed in the small office and could possibly be heard through the thin walls.

Eyes locked was the best. Staring, watching the pleasure take her over. Nothing but beasts in heat, like always.

Every pass of her hot pussy along my shaft drove me closer and closer, my balls tightening up.

"I'm about to come," I said against her lips.

My mouth then trailed down her jaw to her neck. No words needed to tell me she was coming. Her body tensed, forcing my hips to do more work, and her pussy clenched around me.

A few more thrusts was all I could take. My dick pulsed, teeth digging into her neck, hands holding her down as I came in emplosive spurts. I twitched with aftershocks as I licked at the new mark I'd made.

She was collapsed against my chest, our harsh breaths in time.

"Why does it seem better at the office?"

I smiled against her throat. "Because there are people only feet away. The thrill of getting caught."

Her pussy squeezed down for a second. "They probably all know."

I pulled back so I could see her face. "Are you embarrassed?"

If her cheeks weren't already pink, they would be turning pink as her head dipped, trying to hide her face. She rested her temple against mine.

"I'm out of time. Now what am I going to do for lunch?"

I smirked. "I have a granola bar in my desk."

She turned to me, mouth agape, and smacked my stomach. "That's not funny."

Chuckling at her, I grabbed for some napkins to clean us up.

I shook my head. "No. What you're thinking is not." Reaching up, I pulled her lips back to mine for a soft kiss. "But it doesn't change the fact that I do have a granola bar in my desk."

Her lips twitched. "Okay."

Okay. A simple word to describe us.

Finally, after so long, we as individuals were okay.

We as a couple were transcendent.

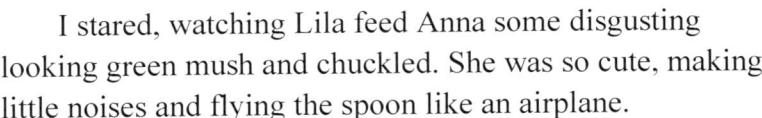

I stared, watching Lila feed Anna some disgusting looking green mush and chuckled. She was so cute, making little noises and flying the spoon like an airplane.

Motherhood was becoming on her. She changed so much, and when I looked at her now, at any time of the day, a genuine smile lit up her face. No more mask—it wasn't needed.

In the hospital, right after she was born, Anna snuggled into her chest. Lila cried. The unconditional love she felt for our daughter, along with our little girl burrowing into her for warmth and love was so overpowering.

Leaning against the counter, watching them, I knew our next step.

I wanted more.

I wanted our family to grow, and I wanted Lila to have more of those moments.

Walking over to the counter where her purse sat, I reached into the pocket where she stored her birth control pills.

"What are you looking for?"

Pulling out the purple packet of pills, I raised it in the air for her to see.

Her brow scrunched in confusion, her eyes watching me as I walked over to the trash can. My foot pushed on the lever of the can and the lid popped up.

I stared at her and smiled before letting go of the pack. The only sound was the pack as it landed, followed by a well-placed giggle from Anna.

A smile broke out on Lila's face. "I want a little boy."

I walked over to her and kissed her hard on the lips. "Can we start when Anna has her nap?" I asked, whispering in her ear.

Pink spread across her cheeks, and she licked her lips. Her hand slipped behind my neck, bringing my lips back down to hers. "Yes, please!"

Chapter 5

Year 4...

"Lila, have you seen my other shoe?" I asked, holding up my one running shoe.

She bounced Jackson in her arms, rubbing his back to get him to burp. "No."

There was a little giggle coming from under the bed, and we both looked in the direction of the sound.

I smiled and gestured with my head to the bed. "Oh, I wonder where it could be. Maybe it's in the closet."

Another giggle.

"In the bathroom?" Lila suggested with a wide smile and a shake of her head as she tried not to laugh at our toddler.

A loud laugh—my daughter thought she was so sneaky.

"Maybe..." I laid down on the floor and reached. "It's under the bed!" Screeches of laughter as I grabbed hold of a toddler leg. "Gotcha!"

She wasn't very far under, and I was able to pull her out. I tickled her sides, making her squeal before reaching back under for my shoe.

Anna smiled wide, little giggles coming from her. "Again!"

I stood and pulled Jackson from Lila's arms so she could finish getting dressed.

"Why don't you help me get Jackson changed and dressed?"

She nodded and smiled, following me down the hall to Jackson's room. We had a crib set up in our room to help with nighttime feedings, but everything else was in his room.

"All right, little man." I set him down on the changing pad and unbuttoned his onesie, tickling his little round Buddha belly and getting the cutest little laugh. "Time to see what you're hiding in here."

In his first few months, he was exhibiting a personality opposite of his big sister. Calm and quiet, he'd been an easy baby, thus far.

Blue eyes and blond hair, he had signs of my nose and Lila's lips. Another beautiful combination of us.

My stomach turned as I opened the diaper up.

"Eew!" Anna said, holding her nose and stepping back.

Eew was right.

It took a minute to clean him up and get a new diaper on his squirming butt before I could button up his onesie again.

As soon as I was done, his little face scrunched up and a screech came out of his mouth, big fat tears falling from his eyes. I cooed at him as I picked him up and help him to my chest.

"Shh, it's okay." I kissed the top of his head as I bounced in place, a technique I perfected with Anna.

Grabbing his diaper bag, I checked to make sure everything was inside, restocking diapers, wipes, and another set of clothes. Then I walked across the hall to Anna's room and loaded her bag with diapers and another set of clothes.

I slung one bag over my shoulder, then patted my pockets to make sure I had my phone and wallet before picking up the second one. Lila came out of the bedroom, and I couldn't help my tongue wetting my lips. A little sundress and strappy sandals, her hair back in a ponytail—beautiful as always.

"We need to get the pool floats," she said before stopping in front of me and reaching up, her lips pressing against mine.

My hand rested on her hip, keeping her close.

Affection was something we craved. Neither of us could go long without it. Touch was much needed for survival.

We headed downstairs where Lila found the floats and put them into the bag she had prepared, complete with towels, sunscreen, and snacks.

Kids in car seats, bags in back, and we were off to my parents for a cookout.

It was only a fifteen-minute drive, but after five, Lila was already asleep. Life with an infant and a toddler was draining, especially since she'd returned to work a week ago.

Work was a subject we hadn't really broached. She loved to work, but I worried it was going to be too much. The minute details of the written law gave her structure in our chaotic lives, and a zone to be herself. But the toll it put on her physically concerned me.

As we pulled into my parents' driveway, Anna yelled in excitement, startling Lila awake.

"I think I need another coffee," she said as she opened the door.

"There you are," Mom said as we unloaded our crew.

She immediately zoomed in on Jackson, picking him up from his car seat as Lila pulled the bags out. Erin was right behind her, tickling Anna's belly and giving Lila a hug as she took some of the bags from her.

The smile on Lila's face, the family we'd become, was more than I ever thought I'd have after the accident.

My own personal heaven.

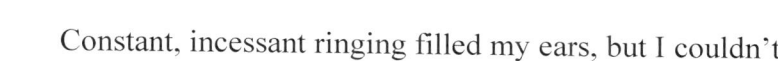

Constant, incessant ringing filled my ears, but I couldn't find the source.

Ring.

Ring.

My eyes popped open, and I slapped my hand down on the phone and brought it closer. The name on the screen was familiar, and I swiped across.

"Hello?"

"*Nathan?*"

I cleared my throat. "Yes."

"*It's Lawrence.*"

The prosecutor from Adam's case.

I peered over at the clock. "It's three in the morning."

"*Sorry to wake you, but I just got the call.*"

Lila stirred beside me, pushing up into a seated position. I put the phone on speaker and placed it between us.

"Lila's here. What call?"

"*Adam picked a fight with another inmate.*"

We looked at each other in the glow of my cell phone. "He's never been able to get over his anger issues."

"*True. He's been getting beaten for the last few months because of his hot head.*"

"What now? Another hearing?" Lila's voice shook a little, and I reached out for her hand.

"*No.*"

"No?" We stared down at the phone in shock.

"*Adam is dead.*"

Lila let out a gasp.

"What?" I needed clarification. We needed to know the details.

If he was truly dead, Lila would be free from the fear that followed her.

"*The guy had a shiv. They found him in his cell, face down in a pool of his own blood.*"

There was no stopping the excitement of the news. It was the justice he truly deserved after everything he'd done to Lila.

The monsters that haunted her were all gone. Dead. Her father died two years prior of a heart attack, and his protégé was rotting in hell with him.

Tears streamed down Lila's eyes and she smiled at me.

For the first time since I met her, she looked lighter than air. No longer weighed down.

Free to spread her wings and fly.

Chapter 6

Year 6...

The week had been long and tiring. Then again, every week was beginning to be like that. Anna and Jackson were in so many activities there wasn't a night in over a month we were home at a regular time.

I rubbed my face and glanced over to the clock with a sigh. The day was minutes from being over, and my to-do list was barely checked off.

Closing up, I settled my desk, readying it for the next day to start the cycle over again.

"Night, Nathan," Angie, my shared secretary, said as I stepped out of my office, locking the door behind me.

"Night." I set a file in her inbox. "Don't stay too late."

"I've got to pick the boys up from their dad's, so no worry there."

I swung by Lila's office and waved to Owen. The poor guy looked swamped as usual. I was surprised that he continued on with the position for so long. Perhaps he, like

Lila, found a sort of peace in the chaos. The more stringent requirements, double checking everything.

He had a little one of his own on the way, and I wondered what Jack was going to do while he was on paternity leave.

Lila cut back to part time when we realized we could no longer handle both our long hours and two children. My income was more than enough to support us, but she didn't want to stop working. Thankfully, Jack was more than willing to reduce her hours just to keep her on.

Twenty minutes later, I pulled into the garage and stepped out. As soon as the door opened, there was a clatter of something falling, followed by little giggle screeches.

"What's going on in here?" I asked, overlooking my children completely covered in white dust.

Lila was standing at the island with an exhausted look on her flour-sprinkled face.

"Hi, Daddy!" Anna jumped up and ran to me, her little arms wrapping around my leg, covering me in the fine white as well.

Jackson followed her lead and grabbed on to my other leg. "Daddy!"

I set down my keys and reached down to pick them both up. Since they'd already gotten me, there was no use trying to stop the spread.

"Just what have you two been doing? You're covered!"

"Jackson did it." Anna wasted no time ratting her brother out.

"Wanta halp Mommy."

"That was sweet of you," I said as I glanced back to Lila, who stared down at the mess looking like she was about to fall over. "Have you two been good today?"

They both nodded, despite the white powder that created a fine misty halo around them.

Anna held up her hand and pointed to it. "I made a turkey out of my hand!"

I chuckled. "Where is it?"

She squirmed in my arms, and I set them both down as she ran off to get it, Jackson chasing behind her. I walked over to Lila and pulled her into my arms. Her whole body sagged against me.

"What's wrong?" I asked as I ran my fingers through her hair, shaking out some of the flour.

She shook her head. "I'm just exhausted. Every movement takes all of my effort."

"Coming down with something?"

"I'm not sure."

I leaned down and placed a kiss on her forehead. "I'm going to go get changed, and when I get back you're going to go upstairs and lay down."

"But..." Her hand waved around.

"I'll clean it up and make dinner."

She tilted her head back, and our eyes met. The dull grey-green that looked at me made my chest clench. I cupped her face and pressed my lips to hers.

"Be right back."

I ran up the stairs, working my tie loose as I went. The sounds of our little ones filled the hall. They probably got distracted in their quest.

In the bedroom, I changed out of my suit and into some lounge pants and a T-shirt.

Back in the hall, I peeked into Anna's room. They were coloring, and behaving—a rarity—so I left them.

I ran back down to the kitchen to find Lila wiping down the counter. "Go relax."

She nodded, then grabbed onto my T-shirt as she leaned into me, her forehead on my chest. A few seconds, then she let go and stepped away.

I picked up the washcloth and rinsed it out before resuming where she left off. Once the counter and sink were done, I pulled out ingredients for some dinner.

Over my relationship with Lila, I'd become a little more self-sufficient in the cooking department. I wasn't going to let her do all the cooking. It wasn't the '50s, and she worked as much if not more than me.

We were partners. Splitting household and parental duties was a no brainer. Especially when it came to parenting—an area where we were both novices. Lila more so than me.

Granted, she cut her work as a transactional attorney to part time, but she was a full-time mom. Thus, the workload of parenting and chores did become a little lopsided.

She joined a few mommy groups online and found a local group where she'd made a few friends. As with everything else in our relationship, we did it together, and eventually found our rhythm.

The giggles and patter of racing children bounced off the high ceilings.

"Don't run," I said loud enough for them to hear.

The running stopped, but when Anna appeared she was bouncing on her toes, still covered in white, with a manic look in her eyes.

My parents called it karma that I had a wild child—Anna was my mini-me. Apparently I drove my parents crazy with my hyperactivity and mischievousness.

"Did you get candy today?" I turned on the water and filled a pot before setting it on the burner.

She nodded so fast it was more like a vibration.

"Can you and your brother go play while I clean up the mess you two made?"

Again, she nodded before bouncing away. "Come on, Jackson!"

It took an hour to clean a mess that should have only taken twenty minutes, thanks to them. As soon as I cleaned an area, they ran through it again, and I was then cleaning footprints.

At another pass, I caught one of them. "Come here!" I picked up Jackson by the waist. He was giggling and squirming as I tried to wipe his face, arms, and hands.

Then I set my sights on Anna. A game of cat and mouse ensued as I chased her around the room, my arms high in the air as I let out monster growls. I was breathing hard by the time I caught her and gave her as good of a wipe down as her wiggly butt would allow.

After that, I gave up. The cleaning service was coming in the morning, and they could get the remnants of the kitchen. It was evident that after dinner I was going to be giving two hellions a bath.

With dinner ready, I sent Anna to get Lila. When my beautiful wife entered the kitchen, she didn't look like she was feeling any better.

I kissed her forehead. "Go sit."

She nodded and headed to the table.

"Mommy, kiss," Jackson said as he stood in front of her, his little lips pursed.

She smiled and leaned down. "Mwah!"

Spaghetti and chicken breasts wasn't the most gourmet meal, but I figured comfort food might be more appealing to her.

I set the plate in front of her, and she smiled up at me. "Thank you."

Jackson already had his hands in the spaghetti, sauce all over him, by the time I sat down with my own plate. Anna was bopping along to some tune in her head as she slurped up a noodle.

I took one bite of my own food before I leaned over and began cutting up Jackson's chicken.

"I think I'm pregnant."

Time stopped for a fraction of a second before I turned to look at her, my knife halfway through his chicken. "Think?"

She pursed her lips. "I'm late, and the smell of the chicken makes me want to vomit. Add in how I've been feeling and, well…"

Three kids? I looked between Anna with her still flour-covered hair and Jackson and his sauce-covered mouth. The thought stunned me, my mind wrapping around the idea of adding another child to our already hectic lives.

I swallowed hard and resumed cutting. "Okay."

"Okay?" She almost sounded confused, but I was honestly still processing the information and that was all I could come up with.

I cleared my throat. "Well, it's shocking and scary, but if we seriously didn't want any more kids, we would've done something about it."

The more I thought about it, the more I was surprised that it hadn't happened earlier. Sure, sex had slowed down over the last few years with our busy schedules, but it was still a multiple-times-a-week occurrence. Lila never went back on birth control, and we never talked about how many we were going to stop at.

"Five's not a bad number," she said, pushing the plate back.

"We already have a minivan."

She nodded. "Anna just gets the backseat now."

A sense of déjà vu came over me. A forgotten dream from long ago.

I couldn't help the smile that formed on my face.

Dreams do come true.

Chapter 7

Year 7...

The house was an odd and eerie quiet. So much that I could actually hear the ticking of the clock above the mantle.

Lila was out with Anna and Jackson in an effort to wear them down some for my parents and nephew. They were going to babysit for the night while we went out to celebrate our anniversary.

Seven years.

Seven years ago, I pledged my love and life to my Lila.

Laying on the couch, my leg ached, stiff from being stuck in the same position for so long. I stretched it while trying not to disturb the bundle on my chest. My little Kayla was curled on me, her soft, sweet breath blowing across my skin. I leaned down and kissed the soft spot on her head and marveled at the miracle that she was. Only three months old, and she already had us all wrapped around her tiny fingers.

My eyes flickered around the room, and I took stock of how much my life had changed over the prior nine years. In that period of time, I had moved from a large, quite literally empty condo in downtown Indianapolis to a four-bedroom home in the suburbs. I was remarried, and we had three beautiful children, Kayla being the most recent, and the house was full of people and toys.

Oh, the toys.

For the longest time, I thought some higher power didn't want me to procreate. But at age forty-four, I had three blessings.

Life turned out much different than I ever thought it would in the twenty years since graduating law school. I'd been in heaven then, but later crashed and burned in hell before rising from the ashes with the help of a broken angel. It took me a long time to understand why. I became a believer in fate, as much as that conflicted my heart about my first marriage.

It became undeniable—I was destined to be with Lila. I had to wage through hell, my life razed, to get there. But now I knew why. My purpose—save Lila.

She was my life, my everything, and she had given me love, life, and warmth. She saved *me* in every way possible.

"Baby, we're home!" Lila called from the garage entrance near the kitchen.

"In here!" I called back, trying not to disturb the sleeping angel on my chest.

My two little hellions—or rather one little hellion and her sidekick—came running in and were trying to tell me all about what they had done. I put my fingers to my lips to shush them as the baby stirred and snuggled deeper into my chest, her face scrunched and her tiny fists clenched onto my shirt. She did not like the disturbance.

Anna was already a handful at age five—and a half, as she would say. She took after her daddy, while Jackson was more like Lila.

They settled down quickly and, in their inside voices, told me all about their afternoon adventures before they were off to play some more.

Lila's lips pressed against my forehead, and one of my hands released Kayla to pull her mouth down to mine. When we released, I saw the wicked gleam in her eye, and I knew she was as excited about the evening as I was. She reached out and ran her fingers lightly across Kayla's head.

"How long has she been asleep?"

I craned my neck to look over at the clock. "Almost two hours."

"Well, she should be up and ready to entertain Grandma and Grandpa soon," she said with a sweet smile. My hand involuntarily reached for hers and brought it to my lips, lightly kissing her fingers. Her lips twitched up into a smile, and she let out a small giggle.

I fucking loved it when she giggled. It was a rare occurrence.

"Just warming my lips up for tonight." I grinned and watched her cheeks flush, her bottom lip caught between her teeth. It was then that I knew I had her, by her telltale signs.

Over the following hours, we took showers in turn, watching out for the troublemakers and entertaining Kayla.

I took the first turn, bouncing Kayla in my arms in the bedroom, Anna and Jackson in the playroom. When Lila came out of the shower, I took my first good look at her in what felt like weeks, maybe months.

Yes, she'd aged some—three kids helped with that—but she was still as beautiful as the day we met. She would always be beautiful in my eyes.

What some considered imperfections, weren't to me. They were battle scars. Not just stretchmarks from our babies and whatever else she would find wrong—all of it.

Scars from life.

We were almost mirror images of banged up. Proof of our fight to live. To be able to stand in the same room together and know we made it—we were alive.

My life wasn't over ten years ago like I'd thought it was. Lila taught me that. Baby steps together, all leading to a clearing I never thought possible.

It was hectic and difficult at times, but filled with our family.

I loved my life.

Our anniversary gifts to each other was a night away from it all. Always-needed one-on-one time. No talk of kids. Adult talk. Remembering who we were outside of Mommy and Daddy.

The hotel was what we were both the most interested in. Dinner could wait.

Check-in had my leg bouncing, agitation and anticipation growing with each second that ticked by. Each second my cock got harder.

I'd been half hard by the time we pulled out of the driveway.

Keys and bag in one hand, Lila in the other, we walked a fast pace to the elevators, both grinning ear to ear.

The elevator was empty when it arrived. The moment we stepped in, we reenacted scenes from years ago at our old downtown condos. I pressed her against the wall, mouth on hers, taking from her.

I needed her. All of her.

Desperate to have all of her attention and give all of my attention.

She reached down and cupped her hand around my cock, making me moan into her.

I couldn't take it anymore.

Luckily, our room wasn't far from the elevators. As soon as we crossed the threshold to the room, our bag was on the ground and I had her pinned against the wall. Her legs were up around my hips and I had her panties pushed aside before the door had even clicked closed. By the time the sound was done, I was buried inside her.

"Fuck!" I cried out. The feeling of her wrapped around my cock was heaven.

Even after eight years together, we never lost that spark. Never lost that incessant need for touch.

I began thrusting hard, unable to control myself. It had been far too long since we'd been alone, and I was blissed out hearing her cry out, full voice, with each thrust of my hips.

Stepping back, I walked her over to the bed and laid her down.

As much as I wanted to come, I also wanted the moment to last.

"You're so beautiful," I said, reaching out and brushing a strand of hair from her face.

She smiled at me, her hand cupping my face. My hips slowed down from their initial pounding to longer rotations, reveling in the feel of her around me.

"I love you." Tears filled her eyes, some spilling over onto the bed below.

My thumb brushed the next ones away. "I love you."

Beautiful grey-green eyes flitted between mine. "Forever."

I leaned down and pressed my forehead against hers.

"This life and the next, and it will still never be enough."

Over the years we'd been through so much. There we were, busy with work and children and life.

There was no more pain, no more fear, only love and happiness.

Forever.

Made in the USA
Lexington, KY
18 April 2018